DIANE SWANSON

ANIMALS
CAN BE SO
SLEEPY

GREYSTONE BOOKS
DOUGLAS & McINTYRE PUBLISHING GROUP
VANCOUVER / TORONTO / NEW YORK

CONTENTS

Yawning,

Snuggling,

Snoozing,

Animals can be so sleepy.

I SPY, YOU SPY

Find who's yawning, who's snuggling, who's snoozing.

...YAWNING...........

Five furry coypu (KOI-poo)
Gather by the swamp.
They yawn and nestle down together
On a fallen branch.

I SPY, YOU SPY

Find a coypu's button ears.
Shh, they're listening—even
while the coypu sleeps.

3

....dozing.........

One lone polar bear

Dozes on the snow.

Its own coat is a comforter;

Its soft paw, a pillow.

I SPY, YOU SPY

Find the polar bear's nose.

It's as black as the skin beneath

the bear's white coat.

resting.........

Three marine iguanas
Rest on rocky shores.
Bit by bit, the hot sun warms them,
Cold from diving in the sea.

I SPY, YOU SPY

Find which long, scaly toes belong to which long, sleepy iguana.

NAPPING

After lunch, a lioness takes a cat nap.

Her cushion—her cub—wakes up first,

Lifting her heavy head high.

I SPY, YOU SPY

Find what the lion cub was sleeping on.

relaxing

Stretched out on a log,
A chimpanzee relaxes.
It builds a nest when nighttime comes,
Sleeping safely in a tree.

I SPY, YOU SPY

Find what the chimpanzee
is using for a pillow.

...snuggling....

Walruses snuggle on ice and on shore,

Body by body

By fat, wrinkly body.

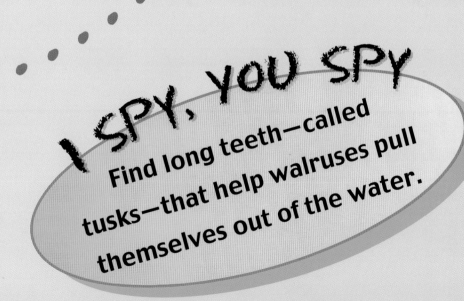

I SPY, YOU SPY

Find long teeth—called tusks—that help walruses pull themselves out of the water.

13

...nodding off.....

Mother great horned owl
Keeps her chick close by.
Her watchful eyes stay open
While the chick nods off.

I SPY, YOU SPY

Find which owl has a thick coat. It's weatherproof to protect the owl—and the chick.

...snOOZing..........

Sea otters float and snooze,

Lying head to head.

In icy waters and cold winds,

Their thick fur keeps them snug.

I SPY, YOU SPY

Find which parts
of the sea otters are resting
above the water.

...slumbering.....

Red fox, warm fox,
All wrapped up in its tail.
It slumbers in the sunshine
With both its eyes shut tight.

I SPY, YOU SPY

Find the fur that keeps
breezes out of the fox's ears.

19

Yawning,
Snuggling,
Snoozing,
Animals can be so
sleepy.

Points for Parents

 Coypu—also called nutrias and swamp beavers—are South American rodents with webbed feet. They were introduced into North America, Europe, and Asia.

 Walruses are large marine mammals with flippers designed for swimming. They live on islands, on sea ice, and along coasts in countries around the Arctic Ocean.

 Polar bears are huge mammals that live on islands and along coasts in countries around the Arctic Ocean.

 Great horned owls are one of North America's biggest owls. They live in a variety of habitats—wherever they can find food.

 Marine iguanas are the only truly ocean-going lizards in the world. They're found on the Galapagos Islands off the coast of Ecuador in South America.

 Sea otters are marine mammals that live close to coasts and islands in the North Pacific Ocean. They rarely leave the water.

 Lions are Earth's largest cats. Look for them in the grasslands of Africa and a small part of India.

 Red foxes are wild dogs that have red, gray-brown, or silvery black coats. They're adaptable enough to live almost everywhere—except deserts and dense woods.

 Chimpanzees are great apes—not monkeys. They live mostly in open forests and wooded grasslands in Africa.

21

Greystone Books
A division of Douglas & McIntyre Ltd.
2323 Quebec Street, Suite 201
Vancouver, British Columbia V5T 4S7
www.greystonebooks.com

Canadian Cataloguing in Publication Data

Swanson, Diane, 1944–
    Animals can be so sleepy

    ISBN 1-55054-837-9 (bound) — ISBN 1-55054-855-7 (pbk.)

    1. Sleep behavior in animals—Juvenile literature. I. Title.
QL755.3.S92 2001   j591.5'19   C00-911248-0

Library of Congress Cataloguing information is available.

Packaged by House of Words for Greystone Books
Editing by Elizabeth McLean
Cover and interior design by Rose Cowles
Cover photograph by Thomas Kitchin/First Light
Photo credits: p. i Thomas Kitchin/First Light; p. ii (clockwise from top) Alan Sirulnikoff/First Light, J. Eastcott/First Light, Thomas Kitchin/First Light; p. 2 J. Eastcott/First Light; p. 4 Robert Lankinen/First Light; p. 6 Jerry Kobalenko/First Light; p. 8 F. Polking/First Light; p. 10 K. Wothe/First Light; p. 12 Thomas Kitchin/First Light; p. 14 Daniel J. Cox/First Light; p. 16 Alan Sirulnikoff/First Light; p. 18 Thomas Kitchin/First Light

Printed and bound in Hong Kong.

A very special note of thanks goes to Dr. Alison Preece, Faculty of Education, University of Victoria, for her guidance and encouragement in the development of this series.

The publisher gratefully acknowledges the support of the Canada Council for the Arts and of the British Columbia Ministry of Tourism, Small Business and Culture. The publisher also acknowledges the financial support of the Government of Canada through the Book Publishing Industry Development Program.